I0741784

Fantastic Scars

I've known Antoinette for over ten years now, and Steve for over twenty. And the passion I have for their work is exceeded only by their's for sci fi, space opera, splatter, gore, horror and fantasy. Which is why I'm so delighted to be introducing this book to you now. Because it is all that and more; it's Steve and Antoinette at their quintessential best.

I first met Steve back in '84 while writing and drawing for "Phantastique", Australia's first ever horror comic. A serious horror freak, Steve was the driving force behind the publication that, when it first hit the stands in '85, raised the heckles of the right wing ultra conservative talk back kings and set the mega leftist feminist community into a frenzy, baying for blood. Unifying those groups into an unholy alliance takes some doing. But, as I was soon to discover, whenever Steve's work hits the stands, that's par for the course. Uncompromising, unashamed, no apologies, no "beg your pardons", Phantastique was raw and unfettered, horror at it's very best. Needless to say the book was an immediate hit, selling out within days. And a legend was born.

In 1991 comic history was made when Steve teamed up with Antoinette Rydyr to form SCAR, the most innovative, most exciting creative team to hit the world of fantasy comics, and one of Australia's most enduring creative partnerships. Taking it to the world, SCAR's art was soon gracing the pages of horror and fantasy books throughout the globe, earning unbridled critical acclaim and winning new converts to the genre. Once attracting the ire of the feminist community, threatened by the potent combination of sexuality, violence, dominance and aggression, their work began to be viewed in a new light - soon attracting a strong following amongst female readers who recognised the empowering symbolism of their work.

And now, finally, after twenty years…
Phantastique rises from the ashes as Fantastique.

A fusion of '40s and '50s pulp, with a liberal dose of spice and spunk, with Fantastique we are guided through the realm of the femme fatale, a "neo amazone" world where nothing is what it seems. Danger and lust combine as monsters take on the most beguiling, the most alluring, forms. It is the realm where the past meets the future, the bestial with the spiritual. A world without limits. A world without restrictions.

No one is safe. No one is spared.
Unconventional, confronting and truly original, this magazine is a rare treat.
Devour it with delight and savour it with gusto. I promise, you won't be disappointed.

Dave de Vries ~ The Barossa Valley

Fantastique #1
Copyright
© 2005-2006
Steve Carter and
Antoinette Rydyr.
All Rights Reserved.
Published by
Steve Carter's
Comic Nasties.
P.O. Box 11077,
Frankston, VIC 3199,
Australia.
www.weirdwildart.com

First Printed: September 2006.

**Second Printing with
Bonus Story and Pinups:
March 2017.**

ISBN 978-0-9876229-2-1

ON THE OUTSKIRTS OF THE RUINED CITY...
WHY OUT HERE, ANITA? WE'RE A LONG WAY FROM HELP IF ANYTHING HAPPENS.
WHENEVER I SEE CLOUDS ACCUMULATING LIKE THAT I GET NERVOUS...
WE'LL BE FINE.
DAMN!
CLICK!
I TOOK THE PRECAUTION OF DISARMING YOUR WEAPON. EVERYTHING IS UNDER CONTROL.
IT'S ALL ABOUT EMPOWERMENT AND SURVIVAL, GERALD. THE WORLD IS CHANGING, A NEW ORDER IS DAWNING.
MS AVRENA WILL GREATLY APPRECIATE THIS OFFER OF SACRIFICE.

CosmiCAstralvamps

ONCE YOU BECOME ONE WITH THE UNIVERSAL SISTERHOOD, ANITA, THERE IS NO GOING BACK!
...AND YOU MUST PLEDGE UNSWERVING LOYALTY TO THE CAUSE.
THE MALE HEGEMONY MUST BE ANNIHILATED!
EVERY EFFORT MUST BE MADE TO CONVERT MORE SISTERS TO OUR CAUSE,
AND MOST IMPORTANT OF ALL, ...NEVER SHOW MERCY TO A MAN, BE HE YOUR OWN SPOUSE, FATHER BROTHER OR SON.
A MAN CAN NEVER BE YOUR FRIEND, ONLY AN ENEMY OR A SLAVE!
ARE YOU PREPARED TO MAKE SUCH A COMMITMENT, ANITA?
ABSOLUTELY, MS AVRENA!

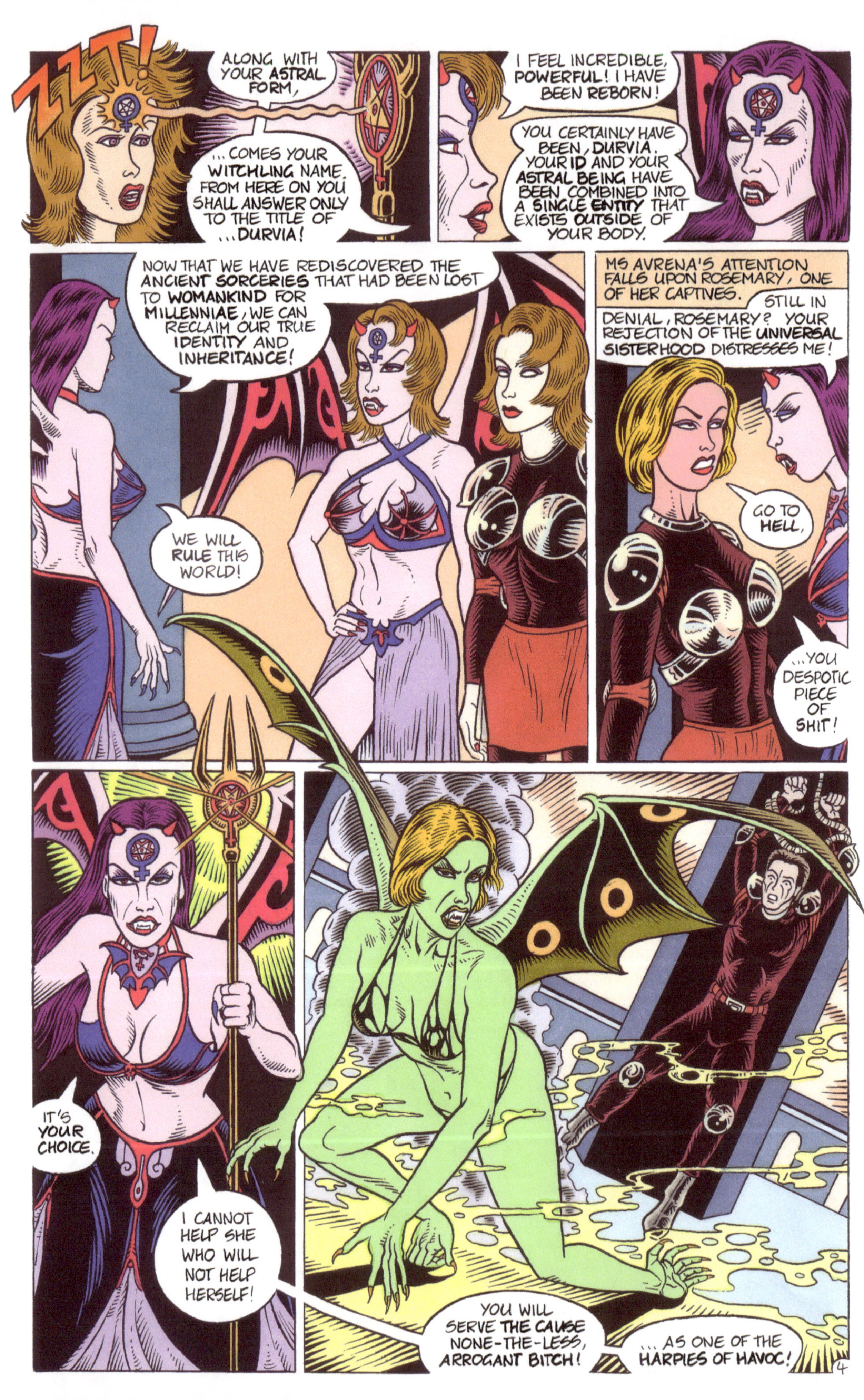

ZZT!
ALONG WITH YOUR ASTRAL FORM,
...COMES YOUR WITCHLING NAME. FROM HERE ON YOU SHALL ANSWER ONLY TO THE TITLE OF ...DURVIA!
I FEEL INCREDIBLE, POWERFUL! I HAVE BEEN REBORN!
YOU CERTAINLY HAVE BEEN, DURVIA. YOUR ID AND YOUR ASTRAL BEING HAVE BEEN COMBINED INTO A SINGLE ENTITY THAT EXISTS OUTSIDE OF YOUR BODY.
NOW THAT WE HAVE REDISCOVERED THE ANCIENT SORCERIES THAT HAD BEEN LOST TO WOMANKIND FOR MILLENNIAE, WE CAN RECLAIM OUR TRUE IDENTITY AND INHERITANCE!
WE WILL RULE THIS WORLD!
MS AVRENA'S ATTENTION FALLS UPON ROSEMARY, ONE OF HER CAPTIVES. STILL IN DENIAL, ROSEMARY? YOUR REJECTION OF THE UNIVERSAL SISTERHOOD DISTRESSES ME!
GO TO HELL,
...YOU DESPOTIC PIECE OF SHIT!
IT'S YOUR CHOICE.
I CANNOT HELP SHE WHO WILL NOT HELP HERSELF!
YOU WILL SERVE THE CAUSE NONE-THE-LESS, ARROGANT BITCH!
...AS ONE OF THE HARPIES OF HAVOC!

4

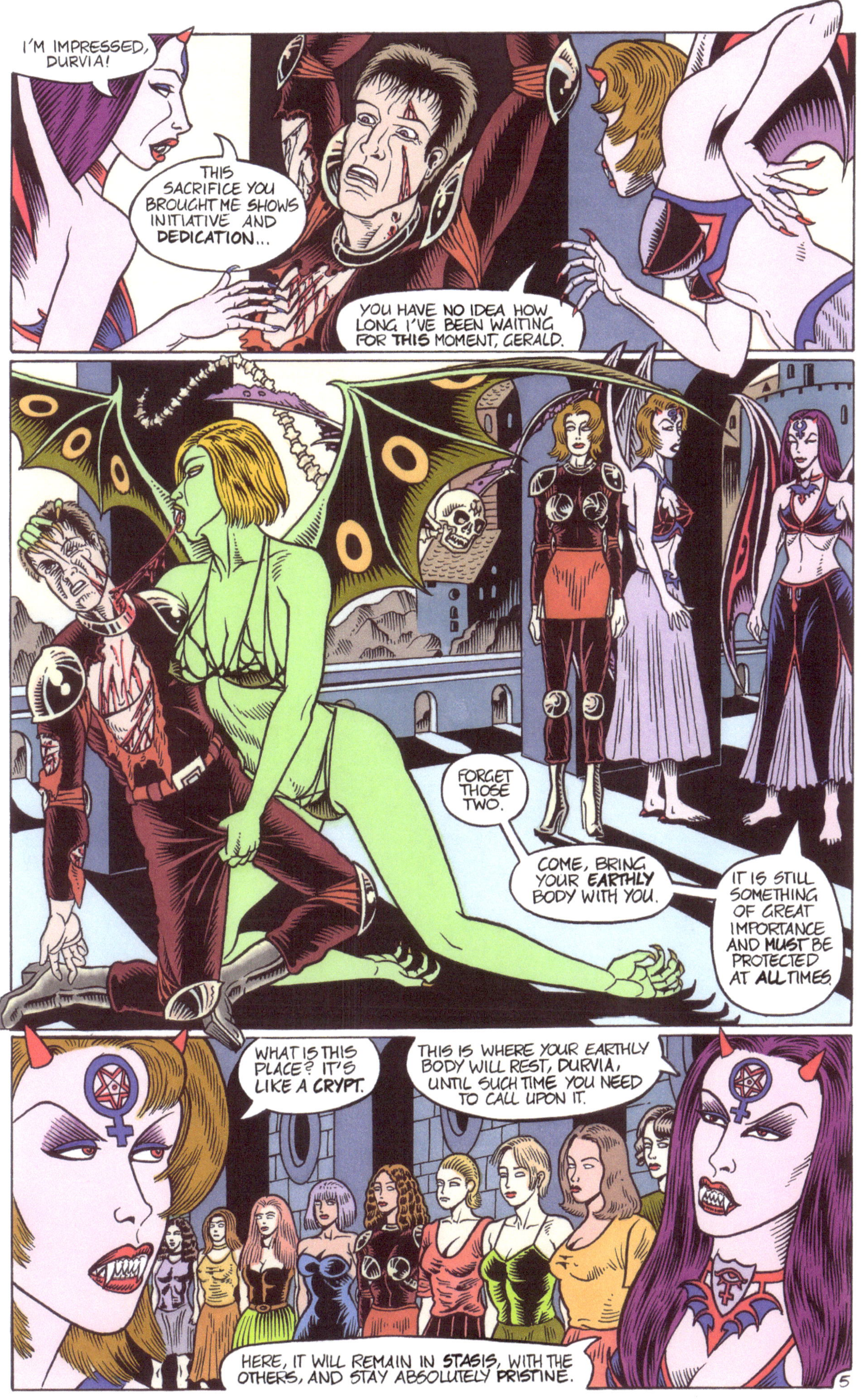

I'M IMPRESSED, DURVIA!
THIS SACRIFICE YOU BROUGHT ME SHOWS INITIATIVE AND DEDICATION...
YOU HAVE NO IDEA HOW LONG I'VE BEEN WAITING FOR THIS MOMENT, GERALD.
FORGET THOSE TWO.
COME, BRING YOUR EARTHLY BODY WITH YOU.
IT IS STILL SOMETHING OF GREAT IMPORTANCE AND MUST BE PROTECTED AT ALL TIMES.
WHAT IS THIS PLACE? IT'S LIKE A CRYPT.
THIS IS WHERE YOUR EARTHLY BODY WILL REST, DURVIA, UNTIL SUCH TIME YOU NEED TO CALL UPON IT.
HERE, IT WILL REMAIN IN STASIS, WITH THE OTHERS, AND STAY ABSOLUTELY PRISTINE.

5

WE ALWAYS TRAVEL THROUGH THE ASTRAL REALM, DURVIA.
IT'S QUICKER AND OUR ETERNAL ENEMY HAS NO IDEA WHERE OR WHEN WE'LL STRIKE UNTIL WE'RE THERE!
THIS IS FREEDOM. OUR PREVIOUS LIVES WERE LIKE THAT OF A BIRD TRAPPED IN A CAGE.
THIS IS HOW THE FEMALE SPIRIT IS MEANT TO BE!
IT'S EXHILARATING!
REMEMBER, YOUR TRIDENT IS YOUR WAND AND A WEAPON. IT'S TUNED ONLY TO YOU!
THEY ALWAYS SEND THE HARPIES IN FIRST!
AT LEAST THEY DON'T COME BACK ONCE YOU TAKE THEM DOWN!
AS THE BATTLE RAGED A SQUADRON SET OFF ON A SPECIAL MISSION.
WHILE THE MAJORITY OF THOSE HELL WITCHES ARE ENGAGED HERE, THEIR LAIR WILL BE VULNERABLE...
...STILL GOT TO FIND THEIR HUMAN BODIES WHEN WE GET THERE...
WE'LL FIND THEM!

DURVIA IS THE FIRST OF THE ATTACKING ASTRALVAMPS TO BE SHOT DOWN...

7

...VOICES! IT'S THAT BITCHIN' C.O., SUZANNE! ...WHAT'S SHE DOIN' HERE?

SURPRISED TO SEE ME, ANITA?
HELP ME, PLEASE!
I WAS UNDER THEIR SPELL, NO WILL OF MY OWN!

BULLSHIT, BITCH!
WISZT!
AAAiiEE!

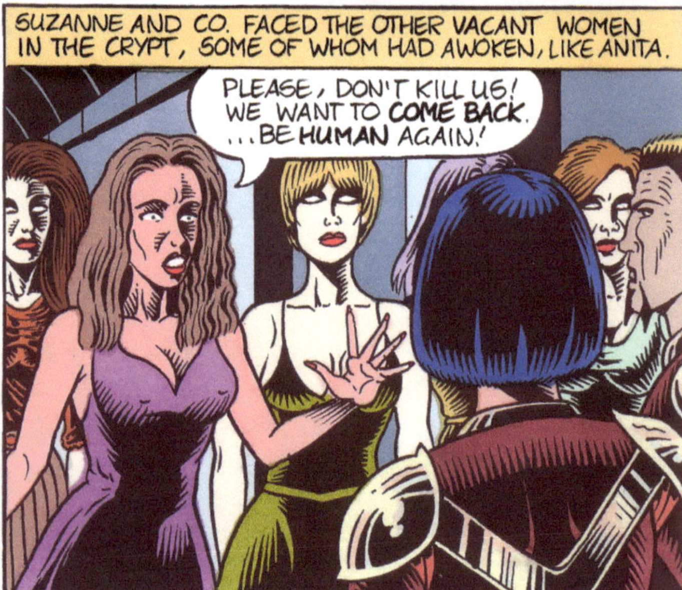

SUZANNE AND CO. FACED THE OTHER VACANT WOMEN IN THE CRYPT, SOME OF WHOM HAD AWOKEN, LIKE ANITA.
PLEASE, DON'T KILL US! WE WANT TO COME BACK. ...BE HUMAN AGAIN!

YOU CAN NEVER BE HUMAN AGAIN! WHAT YOU HAVE DONE CANNOT BE CHANGED. YOU ARE CURSED — ALL OF YOU!
SET YOUR HEAT RAYS ON MAXIMUM!

BURN, WITCHES, BURN!
FIN

FEMME FERALS

" THE VAST NEO AMAZONE HOTLANDS IS ONE OF THE MOST DANGEROUS LOCALES ON THE PLANET NEMESEA. COUNTLESS TERRAN COLONISTS HAVE DISAPPEARED WITHOUT A TRACE
KEEP BACK FROM THE TUSKER AND BE QUIET!
GRAUG!
FEBESSA!
YOUR SPEAR HAS STRUCK THE TUSKER!
YERGLO! LOOK OUT!
"NOT A MOMENT GOES BY WHEN SOMETHING SOMEWHERE ISN'T EITHER FIGHTING FOR IT'S LIFE OR SUCCUMBS TO A BRUTAL END.
2

"NO ONE IN THEIR RIGHT MIND WOULD WANT TO BE STRANDED OUT HERE, VIRTUALLY UNARMED AND HAVING TO FEND FOR THEMSELVES.
KNEW THAT THING WAS UNRELIABLE!
NOW, WE'RE STUCK IN THE MIDDLE OF NOWHERE, MILES FROM BASE!
CAN'T SEEM TO RAISE ANYONE.
GETTING NOTHING BUT STATIC.
OUR ONLY HOPE IS THE DRISHEVI.
WE HAVE GOOD RELATIONS WITH THEM.
I'M CERTAIN I SPOTTED A VILLAGE JUST BEFORE WE WENT DOWN.
IT'S GOT TO BE SOMEWHERE NEAR HERE...

FEEL THAT? ANOTHER EARTH TREMOR!
SURE DID, BARBARA.
THEY'RE GETTING MORE FREQUENT.

DAMN!
DEMU GENGAR!
THEY'RE NOTHING BUT VICIOUS HUNTING TROLLOPS!
THEY'RE NOT HUNTING TROLLOPS BENJAMIN. THEY ARE FEMME FERALIS — FERAL FEMALES!
HUMAN AS YOU AND I, ALBIET PRIMITIVE, AS WERE OUR ANCESTORS ON TERRA.

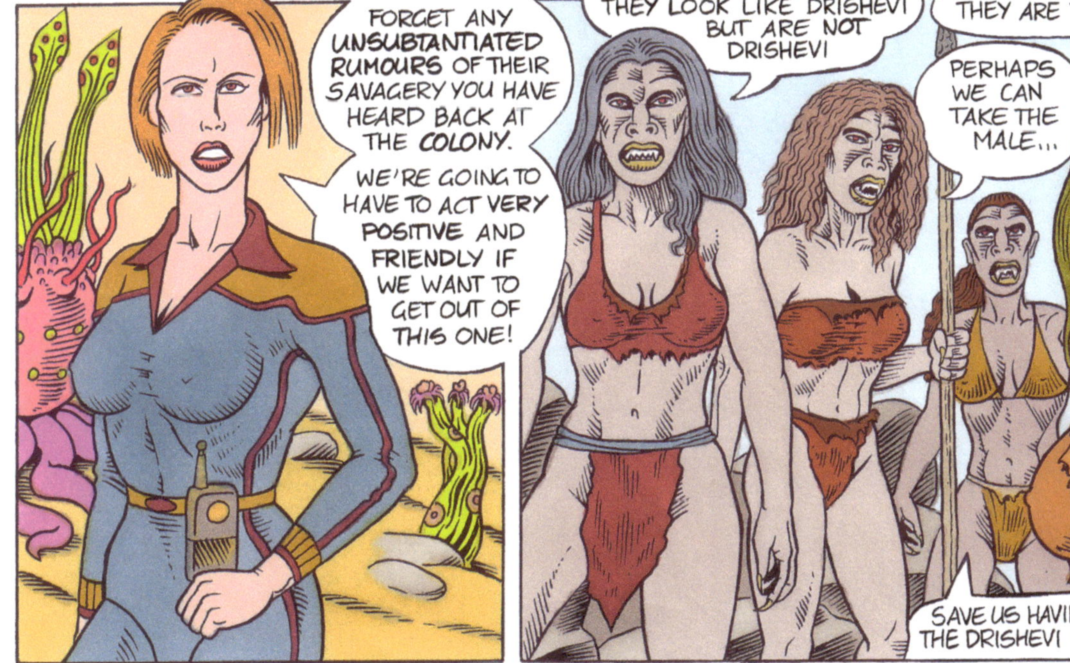
FORGET ANY UNSUBSTANTIATED RUMOURS OF THEIR SAVAGERY YOU HAVE HEARD BACK AT THE COLONY.
WE'RE GOING TO HAVE TO ACT VERY POSITIVE AND FRIENDLY IF WE WANT TO GET OUT OF THIS ONE!
THEY LOOK LIKE DRISHEVI BUT ARE NOT DRISHEVI
THEY ARE TERRANS
PERHAPS WE CAN TAKE THE MALE...
SAVE US HAVING TO FIGHT THE DRISHEVI FOR ONE

"NOT THAT WE HAD ANY GRASP ON THEIR LANGUAGE OR CUSTOMS IN ANY EVENT, BUT WE HAD TO DO SOMETHING...

THE LANGUAGE OF THE DRISHEVI IS REGULARLY USED THROUGHOUT THIS REGION FOR TRADING PURPOSES. PERHAPS THE DEMU GENGAR ARE FAMILIAR WITH IT...

WE ARE FRIENDS.

SHE SPEAKS DRISHEVI!

SHE MUST BE A FRIEND OF THE DRISHEVI!

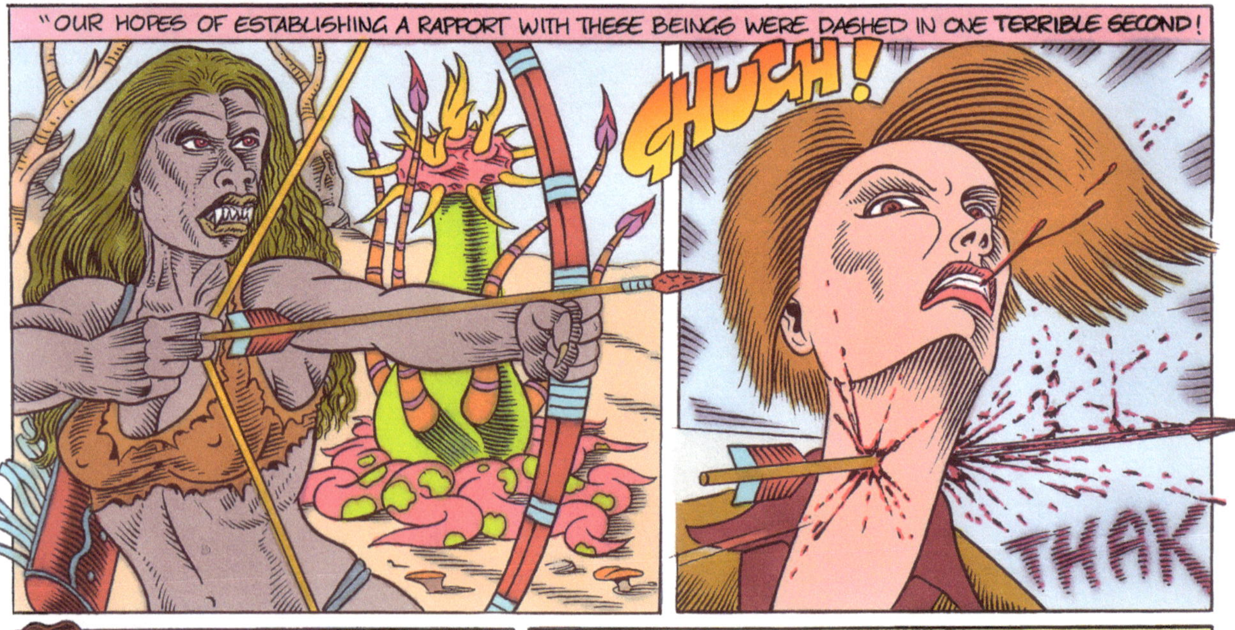

"OUR HOPES OF ESTABLISHING A RAPPORT WITH THESE BEINGS WERE DASHED IN ONE TERRIBLE SECOND!

CHUCH!

THAK

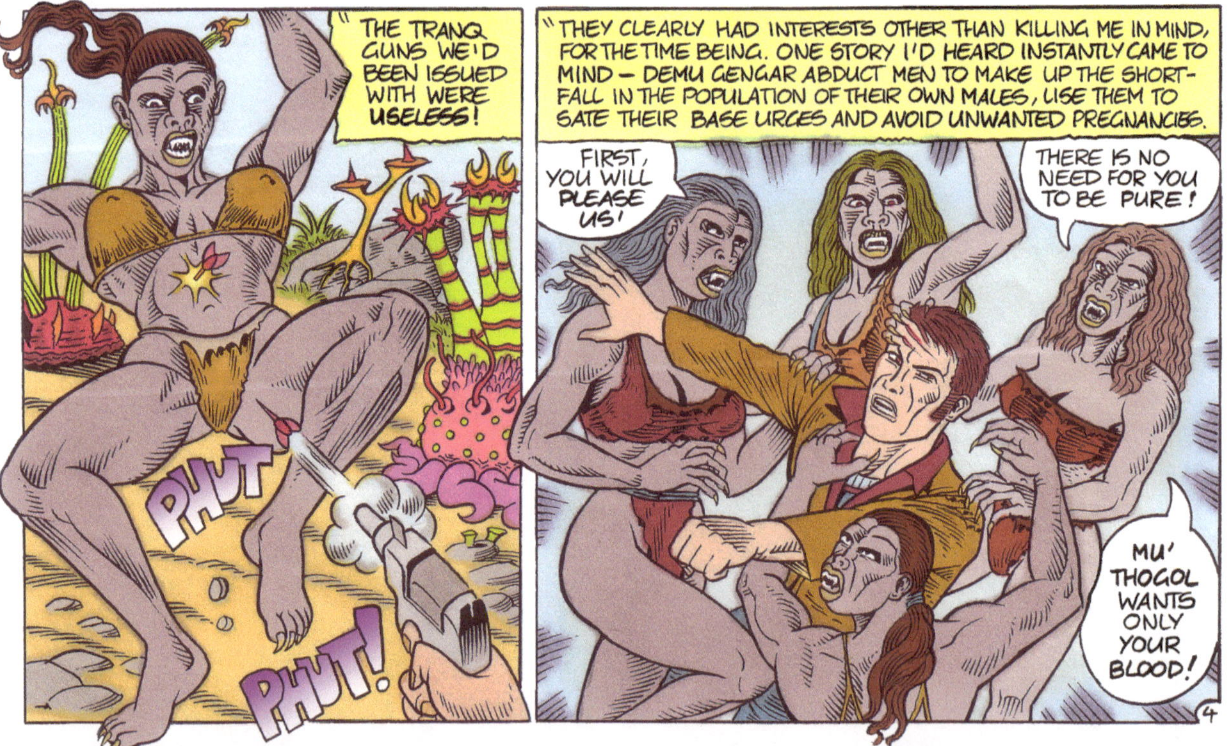

THE TRANQ GUNS WE'D BEEN ISSUED WITH WERE USELESS!

PHYT

PHYT!

SSS

"THEY CLEARLY HAD INTERESTS OTHER THAN KILLING ME IN MIND, FOR THE TIME BEING. ONE STORY I'D HEARD INSTANTLY CAME TO MIND — DEMU GENGAR ABDUCT MEN TO MAKE UP THE SHORTFALL IN THE POPULATION OF THEIR OWN MALES, USE THEM TO SATE THEIR BASE URGES AND AVOID UNWANTED PREGNANCIES.

FIRST, YOU WILL PLEASE US!

THERE IS NO NEED FOR YOU TO BE PURE!

MU'THOGOL WANTS ONLY YOUR BLOOD!

LATER, AT THE DRISHEVI VILLAGE,
TRUST ME. LEAVE IT TO US, WE KNOW THE TERRITORY AND ALL CLANS LIVING WITHIN IT. DEAD OR ALIVE, WE WILL FIND THEM.
SCAVENGERS HAVE ALL BUT FINISHED HER.
THE TERRAN WOMAN WAS KILLED BY ONE OF OUR ARROWS, AZBATA, BUT ONE OF OUR CLAN WOULD NOT KILL A TERRAN!

THE KILLERS WANT THE TERRANS TO BELIEVE WE DID IT!
AND MADE SURE THEY LEFT NO TRACE OF THEIR PRESENCE BEHIND.

OVER HERE, SEBLITA. DEMU GENGAR... AND TRACKS OF A TERRAN AMONG THEM!
IT WILL BE TWIN FULL TOMORROW NIGHT,
AND A MAN BELONGING TO THEIR ENEMY IS ALWAYS SACRIFICED TO MU'THOGOL, THEIR DARK GODDESS.

5

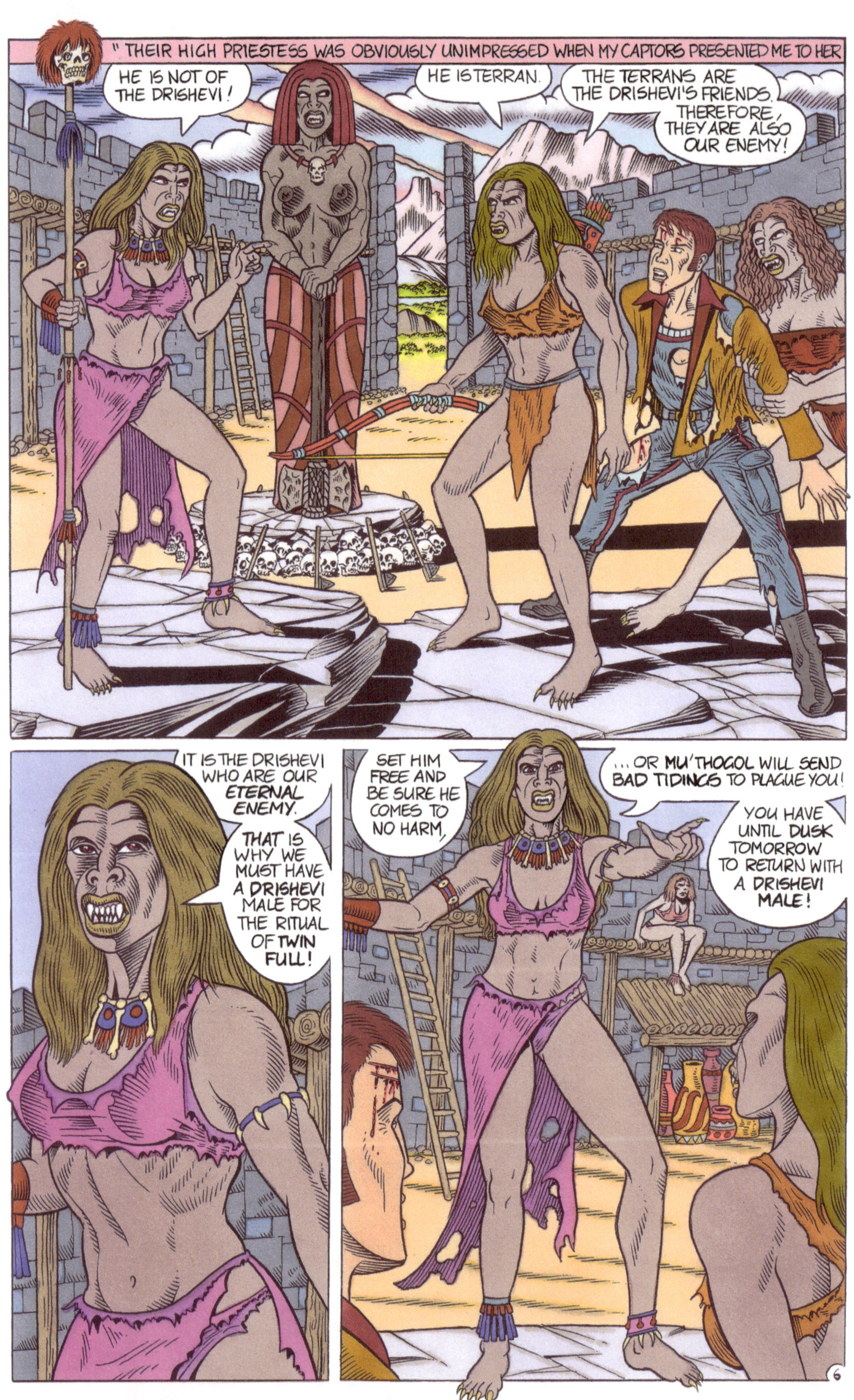

"THEIR HIGH PRIESTESS WAS OBVIOUSLY UNIMPRESSED WHEN MY CAPTORS PRESENTED ME TO HER
HE IS NOT OF THE DRISHEVI!
HE IS TERRAN.
THE TERRANS ARE THE DRISHEVI'S FRIENDS. THEREFORE, THEY ARE ALSO OUR ENEMY!
IT IS THE DRISHEVI WHO ARE OUR ETERNAL ENEMY.
THAT IS WHY WE MUST HAVE A DRISHEVI MALE FOR THE RITUAL OF TWIN FULL!
SET HIM FREE AND BE SURE HE COMES TO NO HARM,
...OR MU'THOGOL WILL SEND BAD TIDINGS TO PLAGUE YOU!
YOU HAVE UNTIL DUSK TOMORROW TO RETURN WITH A DRISHEVI MALE!

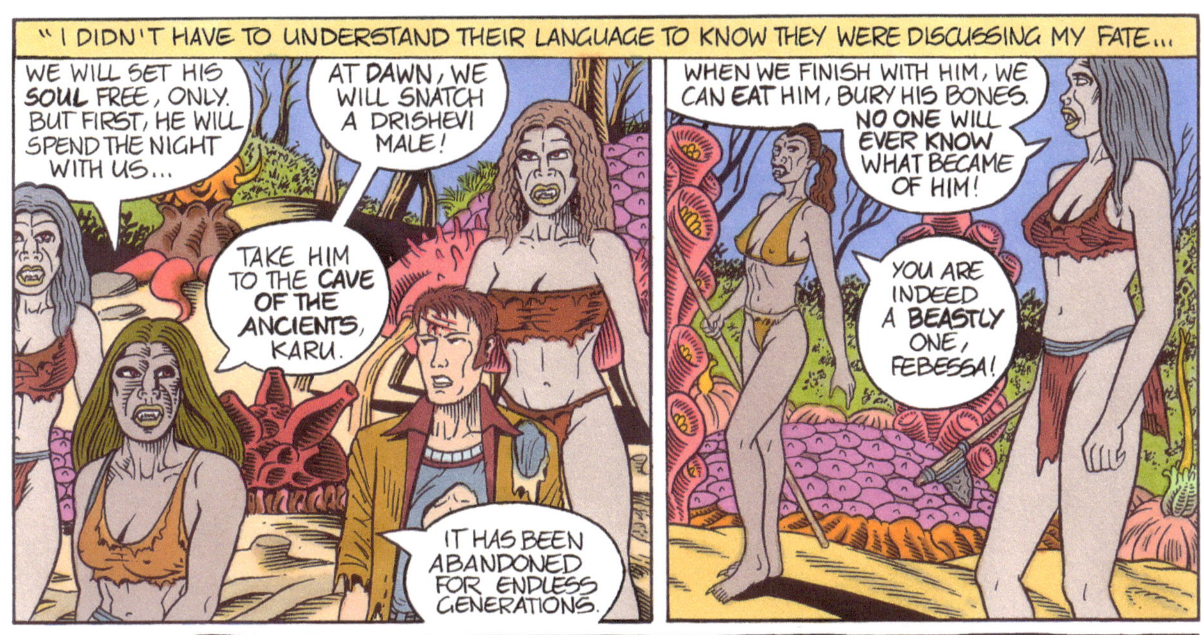
"I DIDN'T HAVE TO UNDERSTAND THEIR LANGUAGE TO KNOW THEY WERE DISCUSSING MY FATE...
WE WILL SET HIS SOUL FREE, ONLY. BUT FIRST, HE WILL SPEND THE NIGHT WITH US...
AT DAWN, WE WILL SNATCH A DRISHEVI MALE!
TAKE HIM TO THE CAVE OF THE ANCIENTS, KARU.
IT HAS BEEN ABANDONED FOR ENDLESS GENERATIONS.
WHEN WE FINISH WITH HIM, WE CAN EAT HIM, BURY HIS BONES. NO ONE WILL EVER KNOW WHAT BECAME OF HIM!
YOU ARE INDEED A BEASTLY ONE, FEBESSA!

"PURE FEAR MOTIVATED ME.
"THE SIGHT OF THAT FOREBODING CAVE TOLD ME I WASN'T COMING OUT ALIVE IF I ENTERED IT."

WE ARE STILL ON THEIR TRAIL AND THEIR VILLAGE IS NOT FAR FROM HERE.
THE RITUAL WILL BE HELD TOMORROW AT DUSK!
GATHER TOGETHER A LARGE RAIDING PARTY...
WE MUST GO BACK QUICKLY.
THEN RETURN!
THAT RUMBLING HAS BEGUN AGAIN, THE GROUND TREMBLES!
THE SPIRITS OF THE UNDERREALM ARE ANGRY TONIGHT!
WAIT! HEAR THAT?
SCREAMS FIGHTING!
...AND NEARBY!

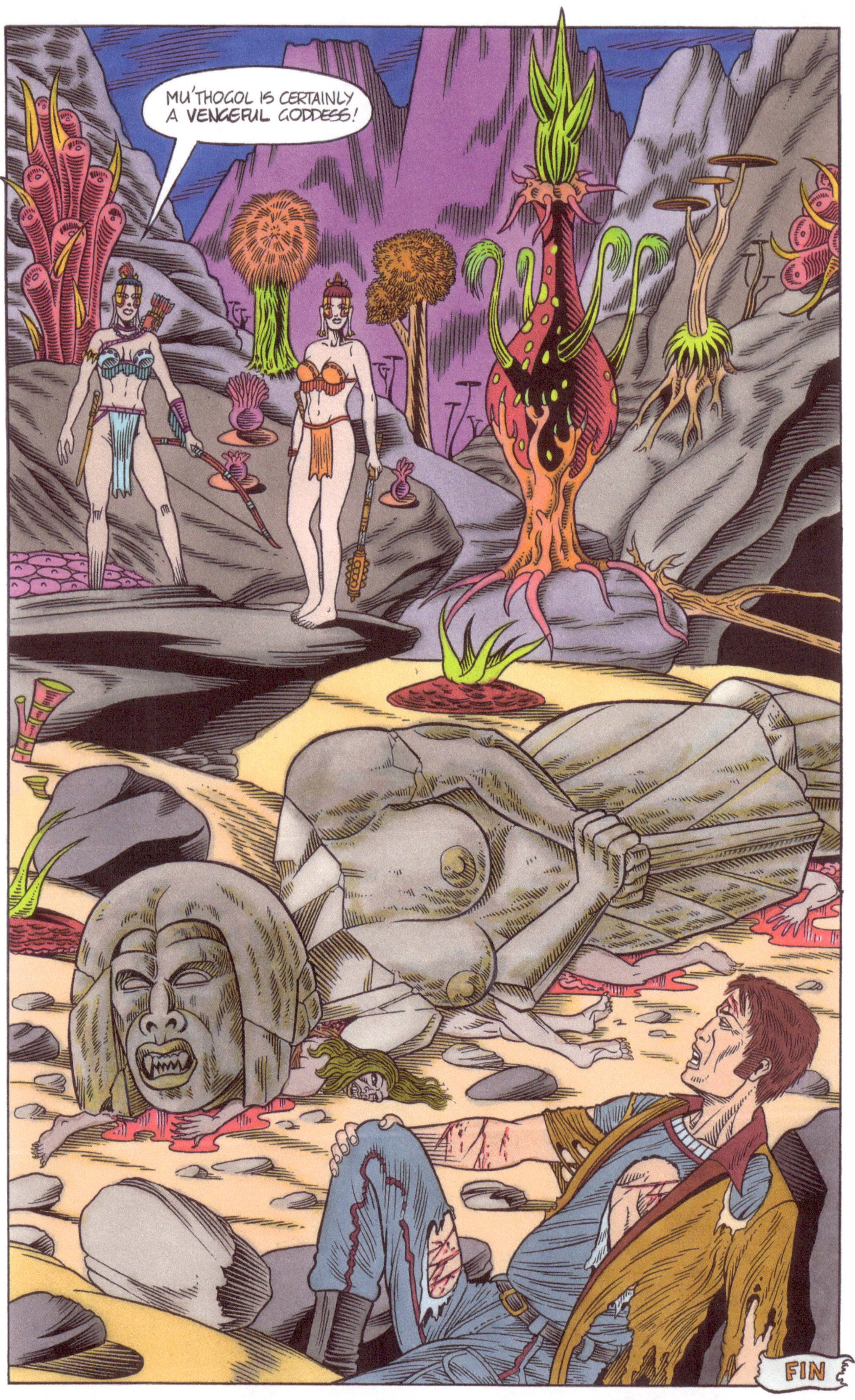

MU'THOGOL IS CERTAINLY A VENGEFUL GODDESS!
FIN

WORLD BEFORE THE FLOOD
IN THE EONS PRECEDING THE GREAT FLOOD STRANGE RACES OF BEINGS AND MONSTERS BESEIGED MANKIND. IT WAS WIDELY BELIEVED THAT DEMONIC INFLUENCES HAD PLAYED A SIGNIFICANT ROLE IN THEIR CREATION — SURELY, NATURE ALONE COULD NOT HAVE CONCEIVED SUCH ABOMINATIONS...
BE YOU ROYALTY OR NOT, YOUR DUTY IS TO SUBMIT, AS DO ALL WENCHES!
THIS ARMY IS IMPATIENT TO SAVOUR THE SPOILS OF WAR.
WE SHALL SEED YOU ALL AND WHEN YOUR BELLIES SWELL, IT WILL BE WITH OUR PROGENY!
THE BATTLE OF SOVYONE
BY STEVE CARTER AND ANTOINETTE RYDYR © 2006

ALL WOMEN CAPABLE OF BEARING CHILDREN HAVE BEEN TAKEN. EVERYBODY ELSE HAS BEEN SLAUGHTERED, AND NOW, THE BESTIAL BLEMMYIAE HAVE OUR CITY OF SOUYONE IN THEIR SIGHTS!
LORD PRIAB, LADY MEBRIB!
THE CITY OF KAIVA HAS BEEN RAZED!
CURSE THE BLEMMYIAE!
CAN WE EVER BE RID OF SUCH ABOMINATIONS?
IT GRIEVES ME TO SAY IT, LADY MEBRIB, BUT IT WILL TAKE AN ARMY GREATER THAN OURS TO RID THIS REALM OF THE BLEMMYIAE.
I AM OPEN TO SUGGESTIONS, ABADDYSS.
ONE SOLUTION COMES TO MIND, BUT I FEAR IT'LL BE AN UN-POPULAR ONE...
LET US HEAR IT. MAKE HASTE!
DOBESCHE.
NO! THE VERY IDEA IS UNSPEAK-ABLE!
THE PEOPLE WON'T STAND FOR IT!
SURELY YOU CAN SEE THAT WE'D BE SIMPLY EXCHANGING ONE HORROR FOR ANOTHER?
THE AMAZOTAURS OF DOBESCHE ARE JUST THE SAME AS THE BLEMMYIAE!
BUT RATHER THAN WOMEN, THEY HAVE A CRAVING FOR MEN!
ONLY A FOOL'D DARE SEEK THEIR HELP!
THEN CALL ME A FOOL. ...I ADMIT THERE IS A RISK...
BUT, THE AMAZOTAURS ARE THE MORTAL ENEMIES OF THE BLEMMYIAE, AND, THEY ARE PARTIAL TO A BARGAIN, WHICH THEY ALWAYS HONOUR.
...WE HAVE PLENTY TO TRADE ~ METAL, TOOLS, WINES... GIVE THEM THE MURDERERS AND RAPISTS IN OUR JAILS, AND DON'T FORGET, MY LORD,
THE BLEMMYIAE MARCH TOWARDS US AS WE SPEAK!

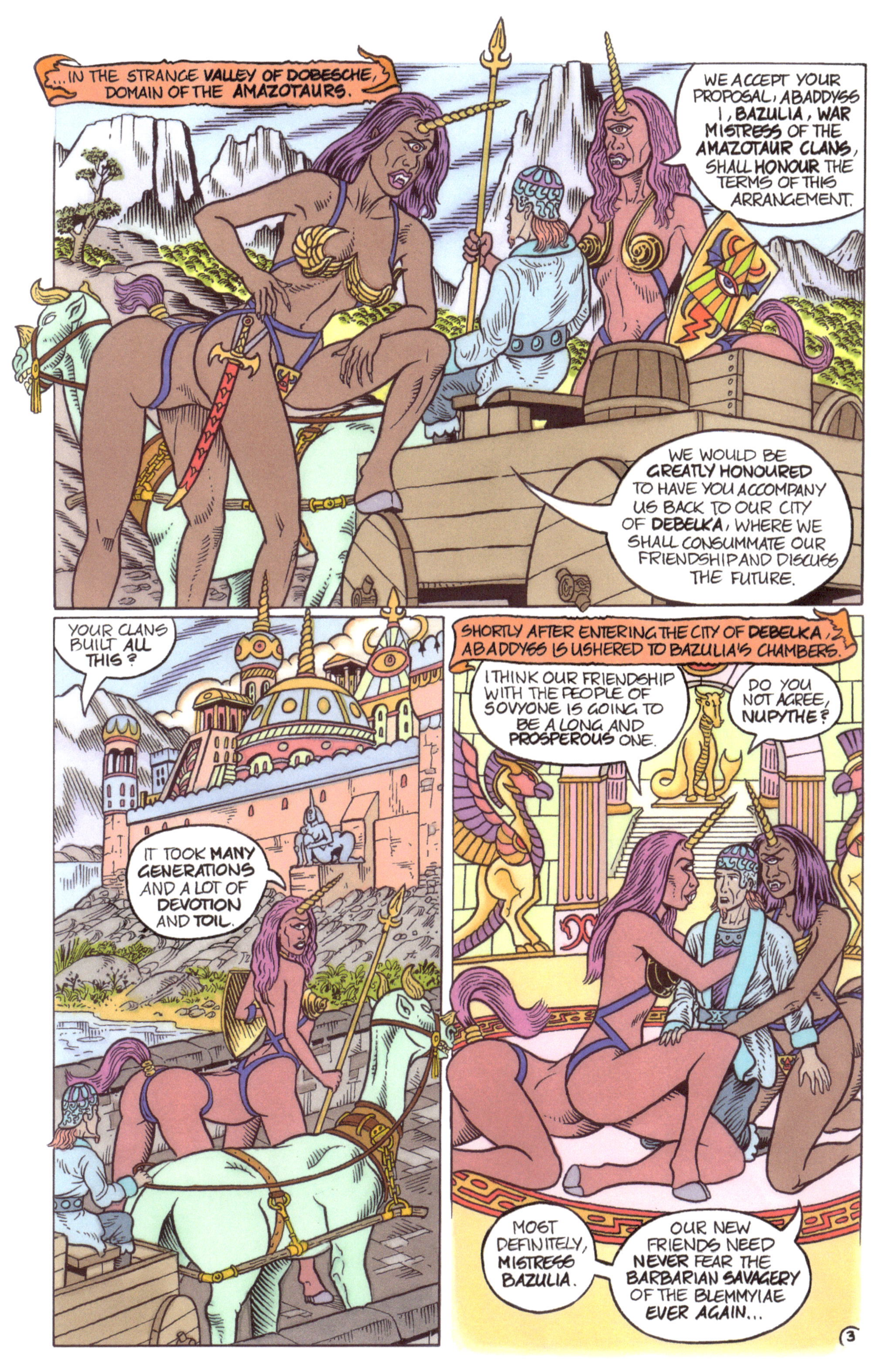

..IN THE STRANGE VALLEY OF DOBESCHE, DOMAIN OF THE AMAZOTAURS.
WE ACCEPT YOUR PROPOSAL, ABADDYSS I, BAZULIA, WAR MISTRESS OF THE AMAZOTAUR CLANS, SHALL HONOUR THE TERMS OF THIS ARRANGEMENT.
WE WOULD BE GREATLY HONOURED TO HAVE YOU ACCOMPANY US BACK TO OUR CITY OF DEBELK'A, WHERE WE SHALL CONSUMMATE OUR FRIENDSHIP AND DISCUSS THE FUTURE.
YOUR CLANS BUILT ALL THIS?
IT TOOK MANY GENERATIONS AND A LOT OF DEVOTION AND TOIL.
SHORTLY AFTER ENTERING THE CITY OF DEBELKA, ABADDYSS IS USHERED TO BAZULIA'S CHAMBERS.
I THINK OUR FRIENDSHIP WITH THE PEOPLE OF SOVYONE IS GOING TO BE A LONG AND PROSPEROUS ONE.
DO YOU NOT AGREE, NUPYTHE?
MOST DEFINITELY, MISTRESS BAZULIA.
OUR NEW FRIENDS NEED NEVER FEAR THE BARBARIAN SAVAGERY OF THE BLEMMYIAE EVER AGAIN...
3

BAZULIA WASTED NO TIME GATHERING HER FORCES. THE AMAZOTAURS CLASHED WITH THE BLEMMYIAE UPON THE STEPPES THAT FLANKED THE VALLEY OF SOVYONE.
S. CARTEZ © 2006
4

?!
YOUR DECISION WAS WRONG, MY LORD. THE PEOPLE DO NOT WISH TO DEPEND ON THE BRUTISH AMAZOTAURS FOR THEIR SALVATION!

EVERY MAN AND WOMAN IN SOVYONE CAPABLE OF BEARING ARMS WAITS AT THE GATE AND BEHIND EVERY WALL,
...BUT THEY WON'T BE JOINING THE AMAZOTAURS ON THE BATTLEFIELD, NOR WILL THEY WELCOME THEM INTO OUR CITY WHEN THE BATTLE IS OVER!

WE SHOULD HAVE FOUGHT OUR OWN WAR, FOR BETTER OR WORSE!
HARD AS IT WAS, I DID WHAT IS BEST FOR US ALL!
NOW, THAT FOOL, ABADDYSS, IS BEING HELD AS A SLAVE IN DEBELKA!
OUR SPIES JUST CONFIRMED IT.
SPIES? WHAT SPIES? WE HAVE NO SPIES IN THE REGION OF DOBESCHE

LADY MEBRIB AND HER ACCOMPLICES SUDDENLY DRAW THEIR WEAPONS.
THE AMAZOTAURS ARE LIARS! THEY'RE HERE TO TAKE SOVYONE!
YOU'RE MAD!
WE NEED A LEADER WHO KNOWS WHAT IS BEST FOR SOVYONE!

5

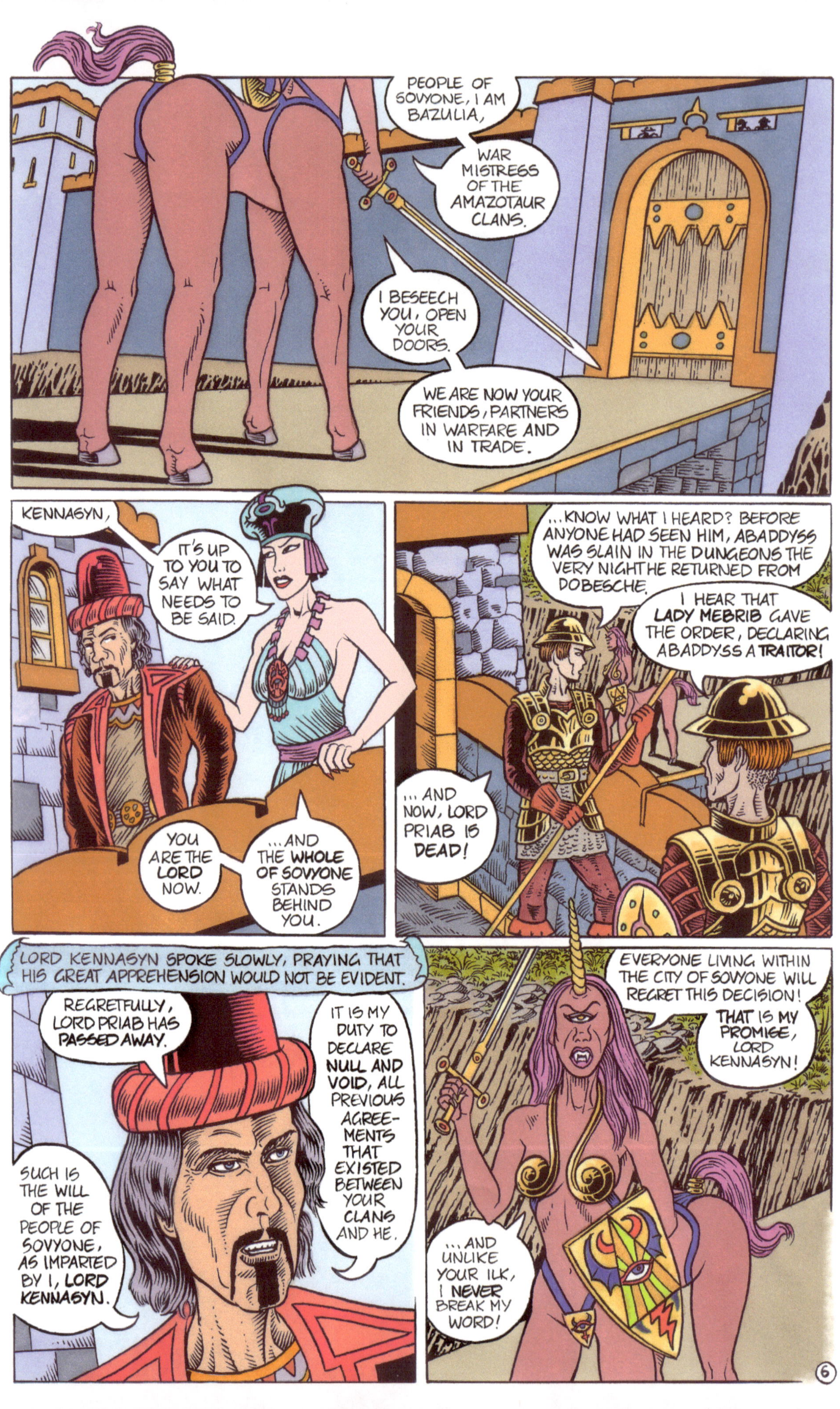

PEOPLE OF SOVYONE, I AM BAZULIA,
WAR MISTRESS OF THE AMAZOTAUR CLANS.
I BESEECH YOU, OPEN YOUR DOORS.
WE ARE NOW YOUR FRIENDS, PARTNERS IN WARFARE AND IN TRADE.
KENNASYN,
IT'S UP TO YOU TO SAY WHAT NEEDS TO BE SAID.
YOU ARE THE LORD NOW.
...AND THE WHOLE OF SOVYONE STANDS BEHIND YOU.
...KNOW WHAT I HEARD? BEFORE ANYONE HAD SEEN HIM, ABADDYSS WAS SLAIN IN THE DUNGEONS THE VERY NIGHT HE RETURNED FROM DOBESCHE.
I HEAR THAT LADY MEBRIB GAVE THE ORDER, DECLARING ABADDYSS A TRAITOR!
...AND NOW, LORD PRIAB IS DEAD!
LORD KENNASYN SPOKE SLOWLY, PRAYING THAT HIS GREAT APPREHENSION WOULD NOT BE EVIDENT.
REGRETFULLY, LORD PRIAB HAS PASSED AWAY.
IT IS MY DUTY TO DECLARE NULL AND VOID, ALL PREVIOUS AGREEMENTS THAT EXISTED BETWEEN YOUR CLANS AND HE.
SUCH IS THE WILL OF THE PEOPLE OF SOVYONE, AS IMPARTED BY I, LORD KENNASYN.
EVERYONE LIVING WITHIN THE CITY OF SOVYONE WILL REGRET THIS DECISION!
THAT IS MY PROMISE, LORD KENNASYN!
...AND UNLIKE YOUR ILK, I NEVER BREAK MY WORD!

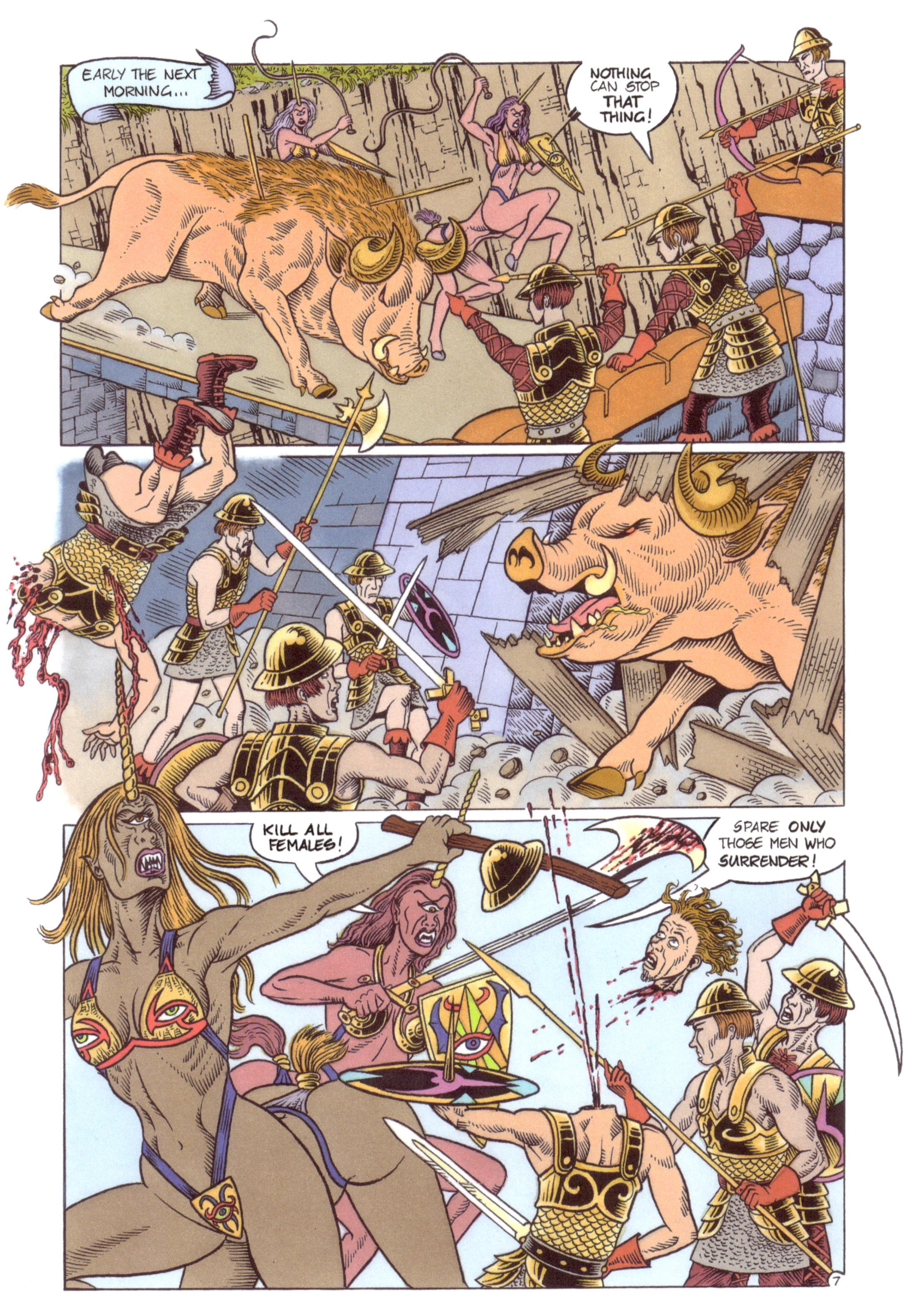

EARLY THE NEXT MORNING...
NOTHING CAN STOP THAT THING!
KILL ALL FEMALES!
SPARE ONLY THOSE MEN WHO SURRENDER!
7

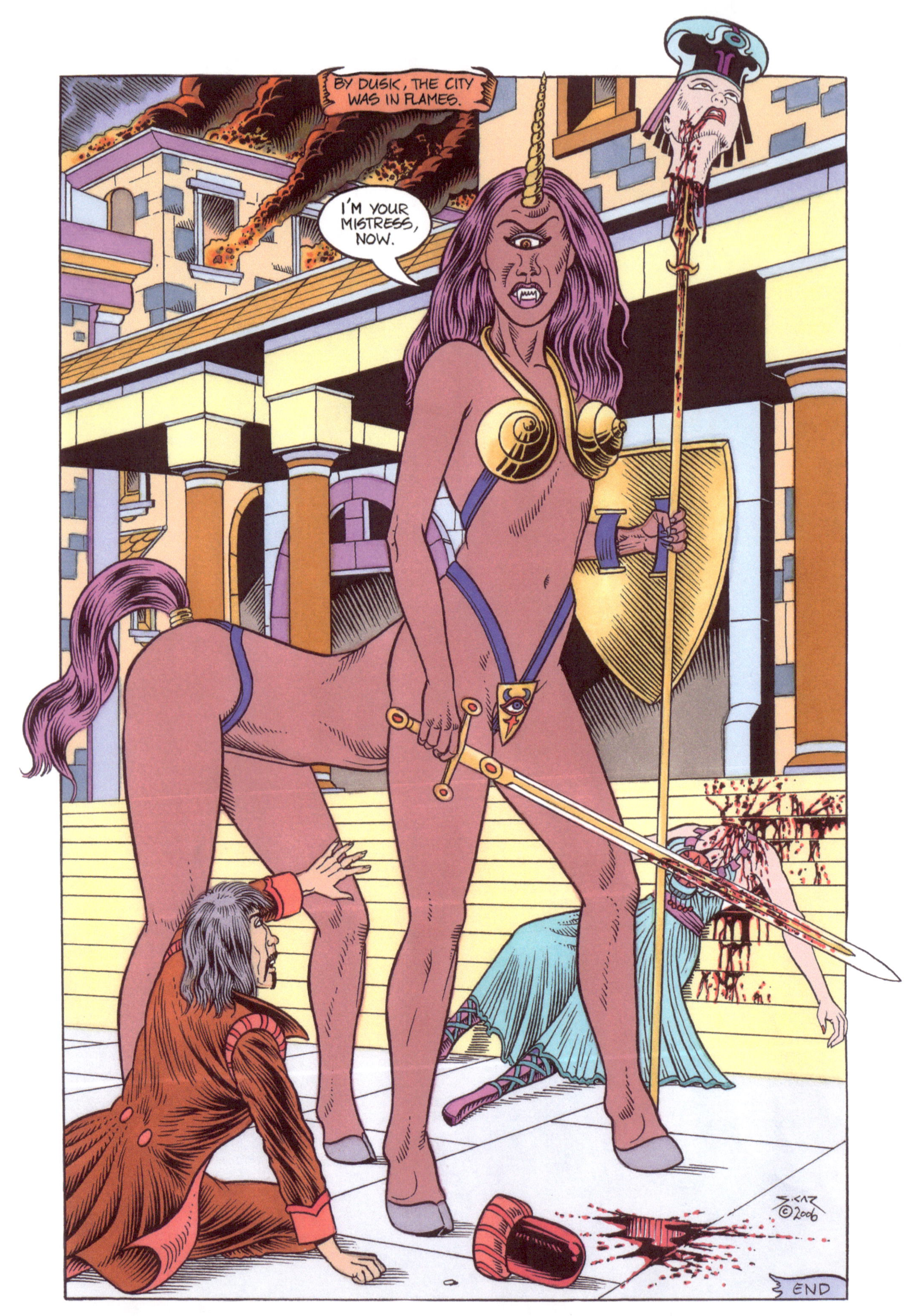

BY DUSK, THE CITY WAS IN FLAMES.
I'M YOUR MISTRESS, NOW.
END

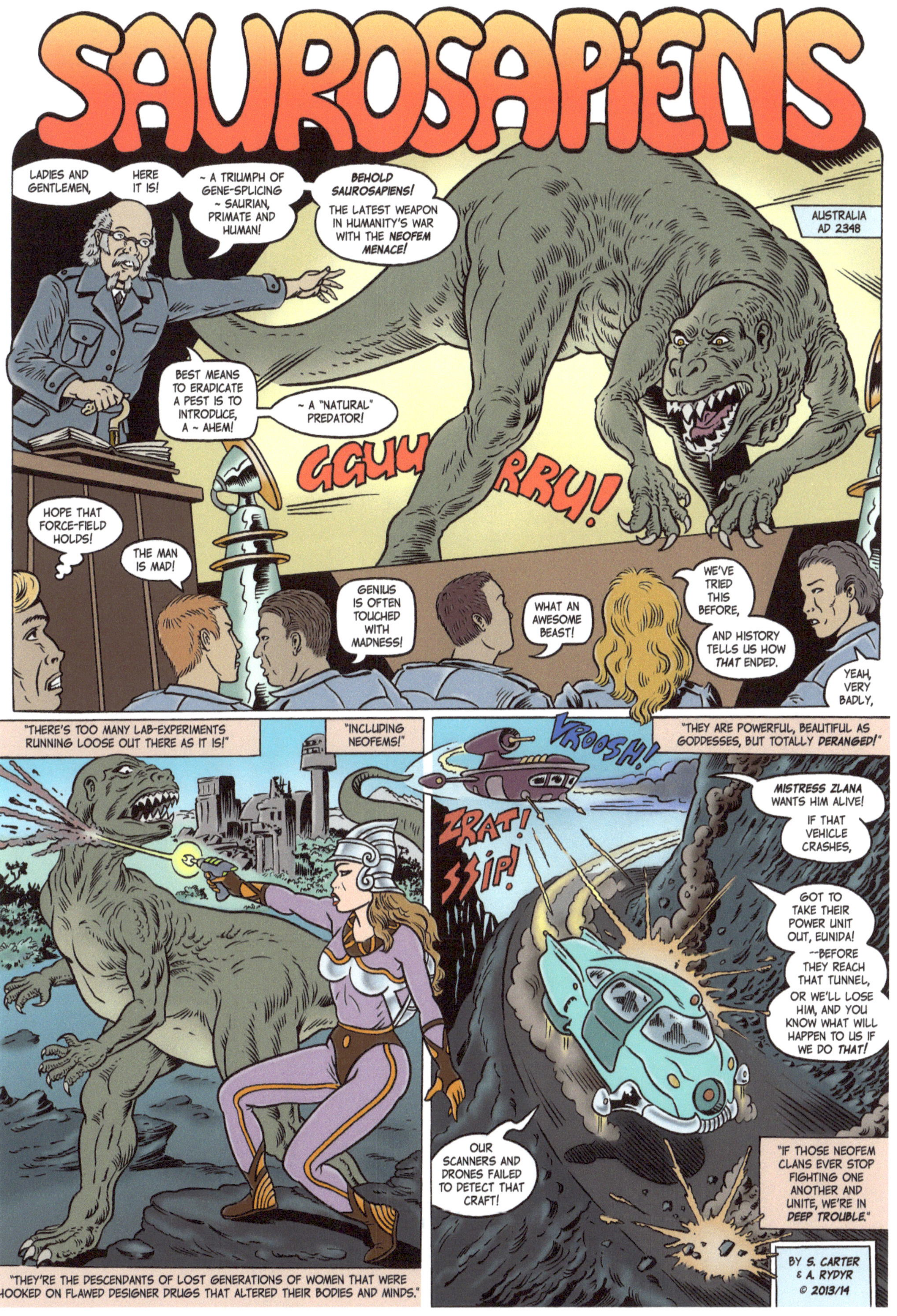

SAUROSAPIENS
LADIES AND GENTLEMEN,
HERE IT IS!
~ A TRIUMPH OF GENE-SPLICING ~ SAURIAN, PRIMATE AND HUMAN!
BEHOLD SAUROSAPIENS! THE LATEST WEAPON IN HUMANITY'S WAR WITH THE NEOFEM MENACE!
AUSTRALIA AD 2348
BEST MEANS TO ERADICATE A PEST IS TO INTRODUCE, A ~ AHEM!
~ A "NATURAL" PREDATOR!
GGUU RRU!
HOPE THAT FORCE-FIELD HOLDS!
THE MAN IS MAD!
GENIUS IS OFTEN TOUCHED WITH MADNESS!
WHAT AN AWESOME BEAST!
WE'VE TRIED THIS BEFORE, AND HISTORY TELLS US HOW THAT ENDED.
YEAH, VERY BADLY,
"THERE'S TOO MANY LAB-EXPERIMENTS RUNNING LOOSE OUT THERE AS IT IS!"
"INCLUDING NEOFEMS!"
VROOSH!
"THEY ARE POWERFUL, BEAUTIFUL AS GODDESSES, BUT TOTALLY DERANGED!"
ZRAT! SSIP!
MISTRESS ZLANA WANTS HIM ALIVE! IF THAT VEHICLE CRASHES,
GOT TO TAKE THEIR POWER UNIT OUT, EUNIDA! --BEFORE THEY REACH THAT TUNNEL, OR WE'LL LOSE HIM, AND YOU KNOW WHAT WILL HAPPEN TO US IF WE DO THAT!
OUR SCANNERS AND DRONES FAILED TO DETECT THAT CRAFT!
"IF THOSE NEOFEM CLANS EVER STOP FIGHTING ONE ANOTHER AND UNITE, WE'RE IN DEEP TROUBLE."
BY S. CARTER & A. RYDYR © 2013/14
"THEY'RE THE DESCENDANTS OF LOST GENERATIONS OF WOMEN THAT WERE HOOKED ON FLAWED DESIGNER DRUGS THAT ALTERED THEIR BODIES AND MINDS."

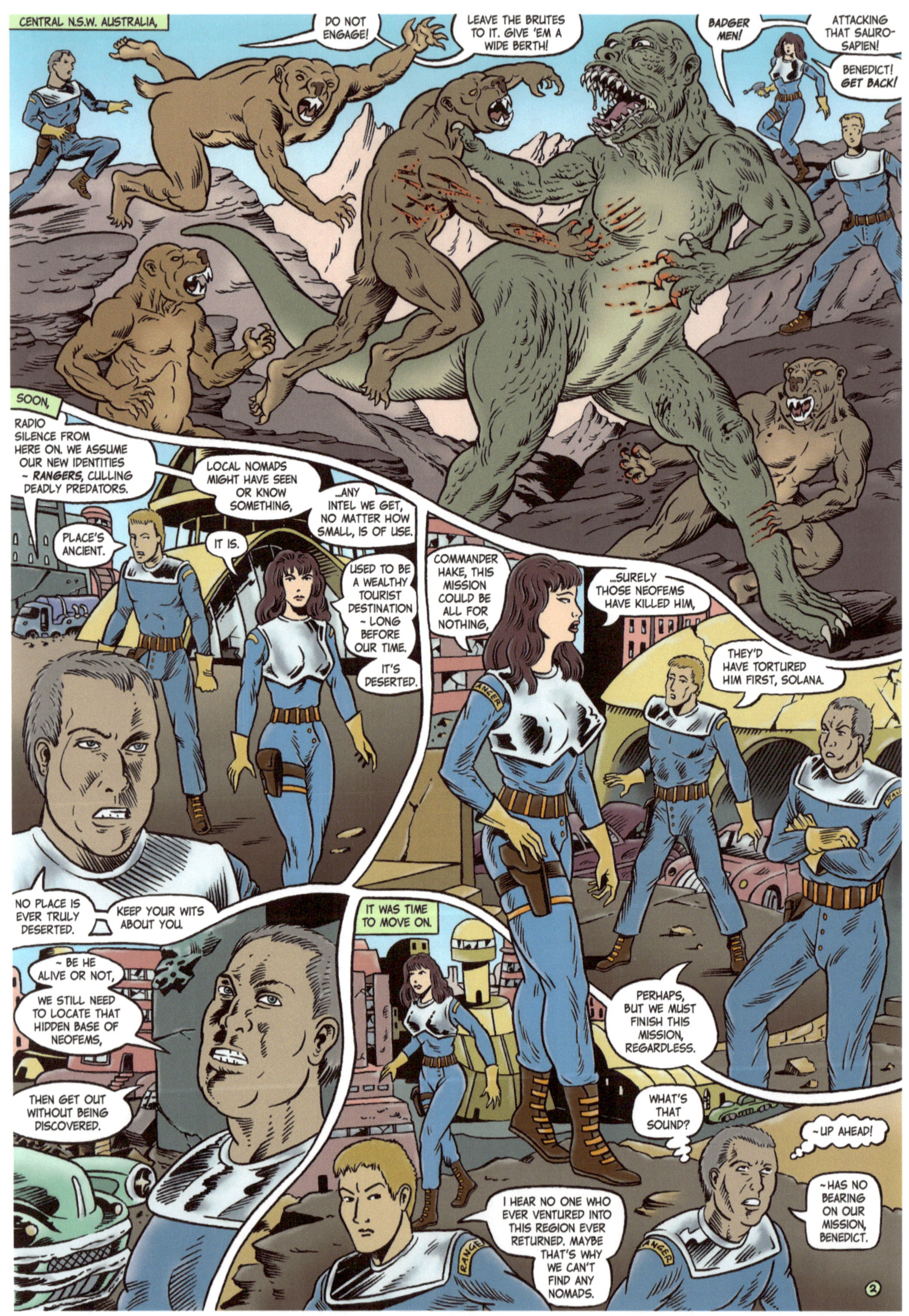

CENTRAL N.S.W. AUSTRALIA,
DO NOT ENGAGE!
LEAVE THE BRUTES TO IT. GIVE 'EM A WIDE BERTH!
BADGER MEN!
ATTACKING THAT SAURO-SAPIEN!
BENEDICT! GET BACK!
SOON,
RADIO SILENCE FROM HERE ON. WE ASSUME OUR NEW IDENTITIES ~ RANGERS, CULLING DEADLY PREDATORS.
LOCAL NOMADS MIGHT HAVE SEEN OR KNOW SOMETHING,
...ANY INTEL WE GET, NO MATTER HOW SMALL, IS OF USE.
PLACE'S ANCIENT.
IT IS.
USED TO BE A WEALTHY TOURIST DESTINATION ~ LONG BEFORE OUR TIME.
IT'S DESERTED.
COMMANDER HAKE, THIS MISSION COULD BE ALL FOR NOTHING,
...SURELY THOSE NEOFEMS HAVE KILLED HIM,
THEY'D HAVE TORTURED HIM FIRST, SOLANA.
NO PLACE IS EVER TRULY DESERTED.
KEEP YOUR WITS ABOUT YOU.
IT WAS TIME TO MOVE ON.
~ BE HE ALIVE OR NOT,
WE STILL NEED TO LOCATE THAT HIDDEN BASE OF NEOFEMS,
THEN GET OUT WITHOUT BEING DISCOVERED.
PERHAPS, BUT WE MUST FINISH THIS MISSION, REGARDLESS.
WHAT'S THAT SOUND?
~ UP AHEAD!
I HEAR NO ONE WHO EVER VENTURED INTO THIS REGION EVER RETURNED. MAYBE THAT'S WHY WE CAN'T FIND ANY NOMADS.
~ HAS NO BEARING ON OUR MISSION, BENEDICT.
2

IF THERE WERE ANY NOMADS 'ROUND HERE, THEY'RE LONG GONE...
HMMM, PICKIN' UP HIGH ENERGY READINGS... ~ CAN'T LOCATE THEIR SOURCE!
SHORTLY,
SAUROSAPIENS?
NOT A SPECIES I KNOW!
SOME KIND OF RECENT, NATURAL ADAPTATION?
AN AIR-YACHT! ~ HIDDEN WITH CLOAKING TECH!
NEOFEMS! WEARIN' JET-PACKS?
KSS!
ZSST!
VIZT!
ZIZT
I AM XARI SUPREME WAR DOMINA OF GLAMAZONIA ~
"RANGERS" ~ WAY OUT HERE?
"GLAMAZONIA", EH?
HALIGHTY BITCH!
WHAT NOW?

SO, THIS IS "GLAMAZONIA". SINCE WHEN HAVE NEOFEMS BECOME SO WELL ORDERED THAT THEY'RE CAPABLE OF ALL THIS?
IT'D HAVE TAKEN DECADES AND LOADS OF FILCHED TECH TO ACHIEVE THIS!
~A MASSIVE HIDDEN BASE! THIS CAVERN'S ENTRANCE HAS BEEN OBSCURED BY HIGHLY SOPHISTICATED CLOAKING TECH!
EVEN OUR BEST SCANS AND SURVEILLANCE MISSED IT.
...WE'RE THE MONSTERS?
IT IS YOU WHO CREATE MONSTERS TO HUNT US DOWN,
~AND WHO CREATED THE DRUGS THAT MADE US WHO WE ARE TODAY!
IT WAS MISTRESS ZLANA WHO TOOK CHARGE OF THE THREE PRISONERS,
THAT DOESN'T EXCUSE YOUR VICIOUS ANTICS!
PLAY THE VICTIM ALL YOU WANT,
GIVE IT YOUR BEST SHOT BITCHES!
IT WON'T BE GOOD ENOUGH!
YOU'LL GET NOTHING OUT OF ME!
PURE SAVAGERY THAT ONE!
JUST GET IT OVER WITH!
YOUR OBSTINATE COMMANDER AND THAT SPITEFUL FEMALE FACE A TERRIBLE FATE.
IT WOULD BE SUCH A SHAME FOR A YOUNG, HANDSOME MAN LIKE YOU TO FOLLOW SUIT...
THERE ARE MANY OF US ~ AND TOO FEW MEN...
I AM NOT ONE THAT WASTES USEFUL RESOURCES. THE LIKES OF YOU HAS BECOME A RARITY...
ESPECIALLY IN THIS REGION.
YOU SHALL LIVE HERE, WITH US,
PERMANENTLY.
ANGER

PROFESSOR GORTHON! SO HE IS ALIVE!
OUR SPECIES' ENTIRE HISTORY, GOING BACK HUNDREDS OF MILLIONS OF YEARS, IS ENCODED IN OUR DNA.
NOW, I HAVE THE MEANS TO UNLOCK THOSE SECRETS AND HAVE DEVELOPED A SERUM THAT CAN ACTIVATE DORMANT GENES ~ AND ALTER THE BIOLOGY AND PHYSIOLOGY OF ANY HUMAN BEING!
THEY GAVE ME A CHOICE, SOLANA; OFFERED ME A STATE OF THE ART LAB, NOT TO MENTION THE ATTENTION OF ALL THOSE GORGEOUS GLAMAZONIANS!
WHY? HOW COULD YOU DO THIS, PROFESSOR GORTHON? BETRAY US ~ BETRAY HUMANITY?
I'VE MADE SO MUCH PROGRESS!
I'M VERY CONTENT HERE.
~ I'M SOON TO WED A BEAUTIFUL NEOFEM BRIDE!
YOU FEEBLE MINDED SIMPLETON, GORTHON! YOU'RE BEING USED!
YOU'RE NOT THE FIRST MAN TO BE BEWITCHED BY THE ENEMY!
USE YOUR BRAIN!
"ALL IT TAKES IS A SINGLE, SIMPLE, PAINLESS INJECTION.
"DO NOT DESPAIR, YOU STILL HAVE YOUR LIVES ~ AND YOUR FREEDOM!
"...IN THE FORM OF A NEW SPECIES OF SAUROSAPIENS,
"~ THE MAGNIFICENT AND SUPERIOR DINOSAPIENS!
BUT YOU WON'T REMEMBER WHO YOU ARE OR WHY YOU CAME HERE."
S. CARTER 2013/14
5

THE DAY CAME WHEN...
YOUR LAB MISFITS ARE OUT OF CONTROL. THEY BREED LIKE RATS... THEY'RE A MENACE!
THEY DO NOT RESPOND TO DISCIPLINE, CANNOT BE TRAINED.
YOU LIED! ~ YOUR SERVICES ARE NO LONGER REQUIRED!
AS WE PROMISED, WE WILL PRESENT YOU WITH A WIFE. MORE SO, YOU CAN HAVE A HAREM! SINCE YOU'RE SO FOND OF YOUR LAB EXPERIMENTS, A HEALTHY BROOD OF BADGER GIRLS IS MORE THAN APPROPRIATE FOR YOU!
YOU'D BETTER PLEASE THEM MORE THAN YOU DID US,
~ OR THEY'LL BADGER YOU TO DEATH!
S. CARTER A. RYDYR
© 2013/16
FIN

www.weirdwildart.com

Scaz © 2006

If you enjoyed this book by SCAR, have a look at their other titles and please consider writing a review. Thanks!

WEIRD WILD WEST

A New Novel by Carter Rydyr & Ethan Somerville

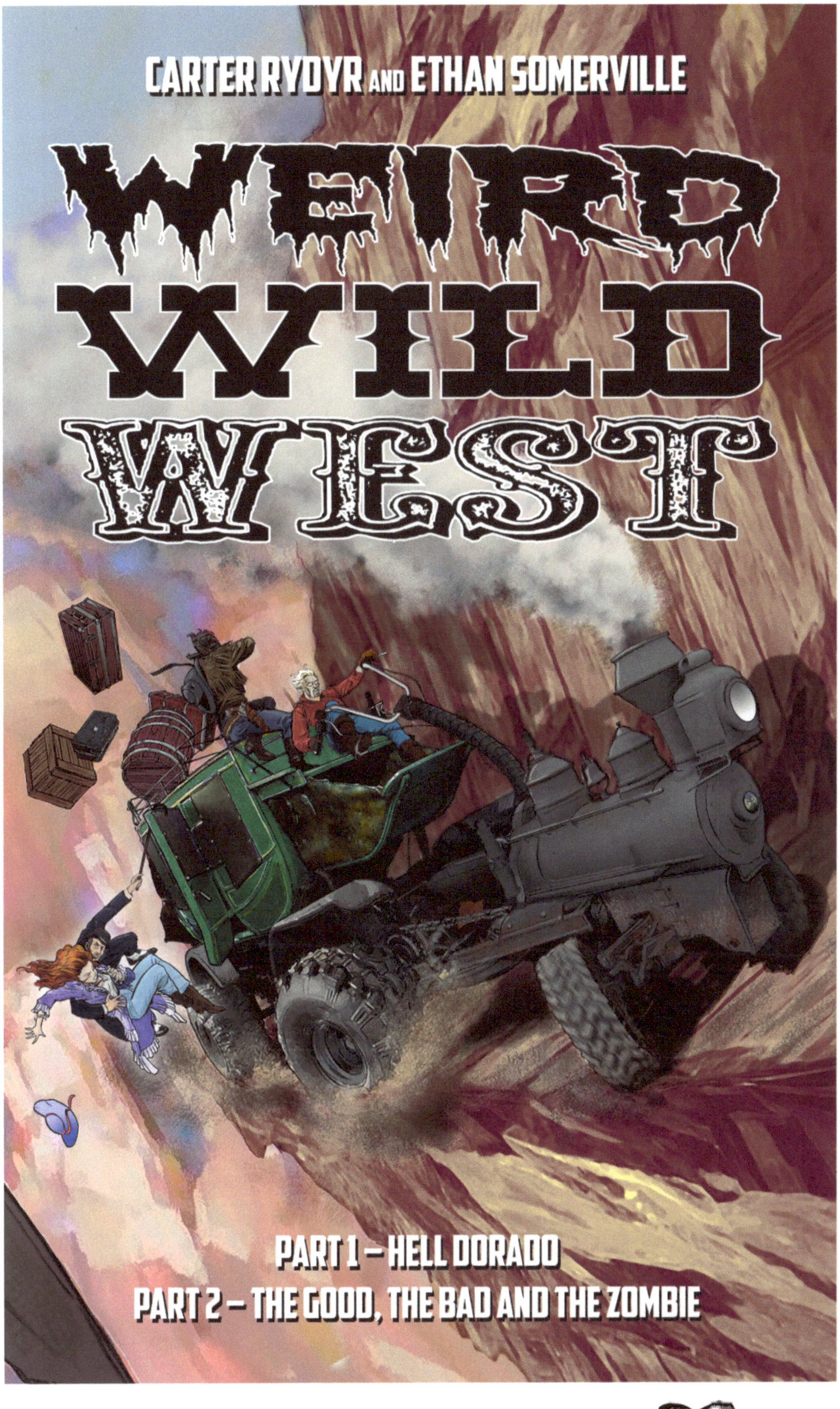

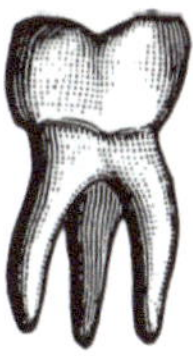

Imagine a wild west that isn't just full of cowboys and outlaws, saloon girls and gamblers. Imagine a wild west that isn't just cacti, tumbleweeds and rolling desert as far as the eye can see. Imagine a wild west of mechanical horses, mutant killer plants, flying dinosaurs, headless indians and fearsome zombie gunslingers hell-bent on revenge.

Imagine the Weird Wild West.

Six colourful characters, some not entirely human, embark on a perilous journey south from Sunbleached Plains to Kellyville. A dapper dentist, a southern belle, a wealthy madam, a retired banker turned gambler, an orphaned boy and a travelling body-parts salesman all trade their various stories to pass the time.

Driving the carriage is one Zeke "the Freak" Sarandon, a retired soldier with more than one strange, nervous habit. Although he is an experienced traveller, and the only one insane enough to take the most direct route south, even he cannot prevent his passengers from each meeting their grisly demise, one by one.

Hot on the trail of the coach, astride an ancient mechanical horse blowing sparks and belching out toxic clouds of smoke, is a zombie gunslinger, the risen corpse of a murdered prospector.

For on the carriage is the one who killed him, and he must have his horrible, bloody revenge.

Bizarro Pulp Press
an imprint of JournalStone Publishing.

Published 2018

ISBN: 978-1-947654-40-2

MORE BOOKS BY S.C.A.R.

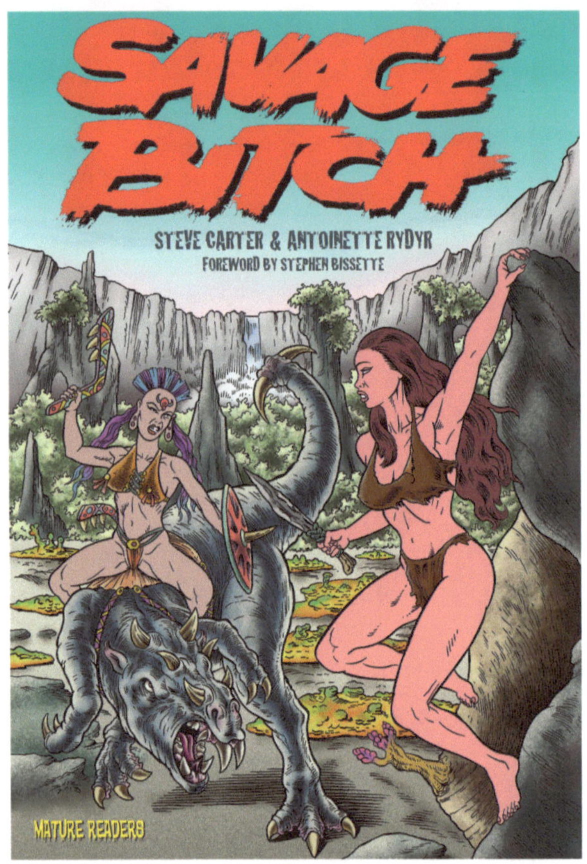

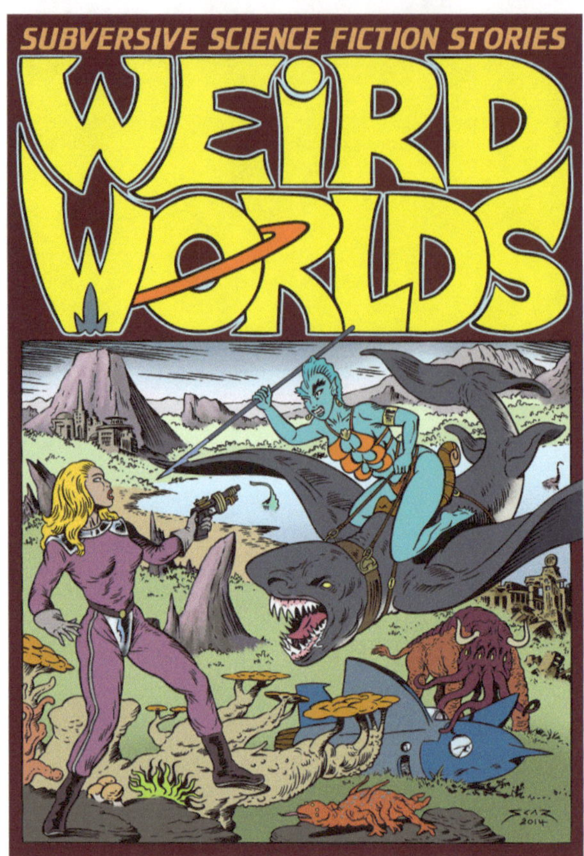

Savage Bitch: ISBN 978-0987622907
Phantastique: ISBN 978-0987622938

Weird Worlds: ISBN 978-0987622914
Fantastique: ISBN 978-0987622921

www.weirdwildart.com

MORE BOOKS BY S.C.A.R.

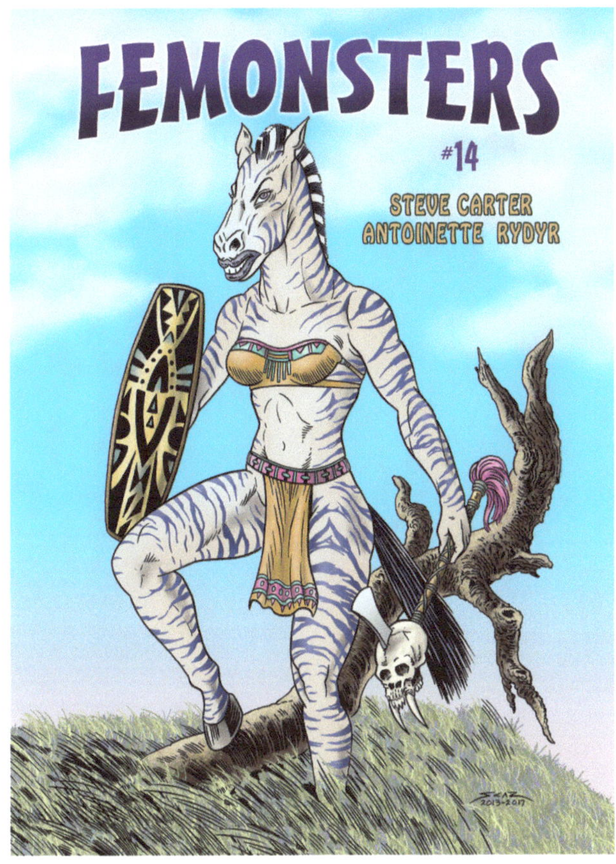

Femonsters #14: ISBN 978-0987622969
Bestiary of Monstruum: ISBN 978-0987622945

New World Disorder: ISBN 978-0987622976
Weird Sex Fantasy: ISBN 978-0987622952

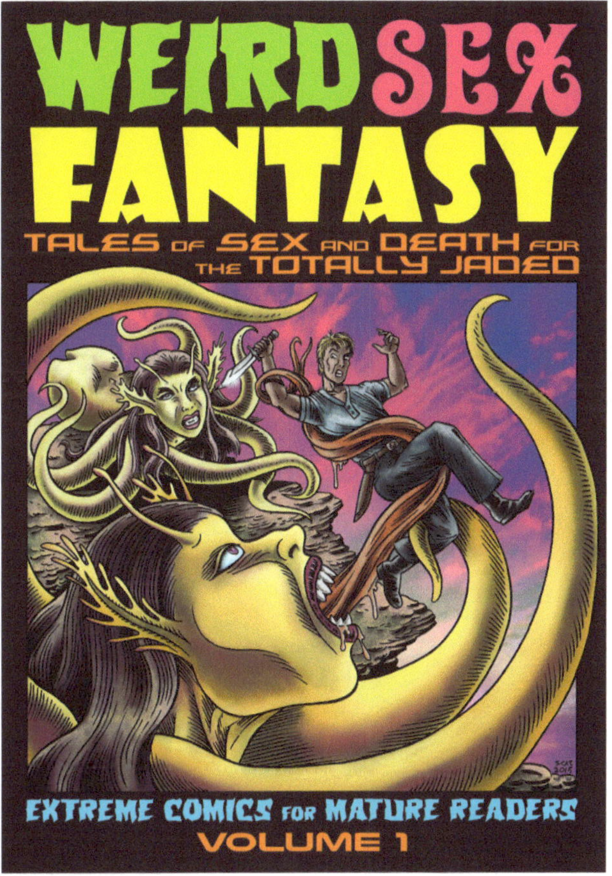

www.weirdwildart.com